This book is dedicated to all the children who I've had the pleasure of teaching, and to all the children who will read this book.

And to my mom Denise Canada; Thank you for showing me by example, that I too, could be a published author.

Tamia Peterson is a Special Education teacher living and teaching in the Washington, D.C. / Northern Virginia area. She believes in honoring the humanity in ALL Children. She has a deep passion for reading, writing and traveling. Mya's Magic Methods is her first book.

Published in association with Bear With Us Productions

Illustration by Martynas Marchiusm
Graphic design by Katie Owens

www.justbearwithus.com

Mya's Magic Methods

Written by Tamia Peterson

Illustrated by Martynas Marchiusm

BEAR W!TH US ©
PRODUCTIONS

Mya was having a bad day.

She didn't sleep well, so she woke up feeling tired.

She was so tired that she didn't want her breakfast.

"Come on, honey. Have a little bit," said her mom.

That made Mya feel tired and mad.

"I don't want it!" she shouted,

and shoved her bowl of cereal away.

At school, Mya couldn't understand the math lesson.
She didn't know what she was supposed to do.
That made her feel mad and worried.

Mya's friend Isabella laughed at her.

"Mya, that's easy!" she said.

That made Mya feel embarrassed and mad again.
She broke Isabella's pencil in half.

Mya was tired, mad, worried and embarrassed.

When Mya got home, her mom asked,

"How was school, sweetie?"

"I don't want to talk about it," snapped Mya.

Her mom looked hurt.

That made Mya feel sad. But she didn't know what to do.

Mya ran to her room. Her feelings were too much for her.
She threw herself on her bed, and cried and cried and cried.

"Why are you crying, Mya,"
said a tiny voice, right by her ear.

Mya looked around. She couldn't see anyone there.

"I'm here," said the tiny voice.

Mya turned her head very slowly, and saw...

...a sparkling fairy, no bigger than her little finger.

Mya rubbed her eyes. "Are you real?" she asked.

"I'm pretty sure I am," replied the fairy.

"Are you going to give me a wish?" asked Mya.
The fairy laughed. It sounded like tiny bells.
"What would you wish for?" she asked.

Mya thought hard. "I'd like to be happy.
Not mad, or worried, or sad."

"Well, I can't promise to make you happy all
the time, Mya," replied the fairy, "but I can give you
something to help you when you're having trouble
with your feelings."

"What is it?!" asked Mya.
She thought it may be a magic potion for happiness, or a magic cloak for cleverness, or a magic spell to stop her worrying, or being mad.

"Look on your bed," the fairy told her.
Excited, Mya looked and saw... a backpack.
"Oh," she said. "A backpack. Um... thank you?"

The fairy laughed her bell—like laugh again. "This is not just any backpack, Mya. This is a Magic Methods backpack."

Mya was confused. "What are 'Methods'?" she asked, frowning

"They are ways of dealing with feelings. You know when your feelings are so strong you don 't know what to do?"

"Uh–huh," Mya replied. She knew exactly what that was like.

"Well, that's when you get a Method out of your backpack.
It will help you to deal with the feeling."
"Okay," said Mya. "Thanks. I guess."

"Why not give it a try?" suggested the fairy.
"Right now, I bet you're feeling disappointed, right?"

Mya felt embarrassed all over again. She reached into
the backpack and pulled out a shining gold card.

FEELING DISAPPOINTED?
STOP AND THINK ABOUT IT said the card.

Mya thought about it. She had hoped the fairy
would make everything better with a magic spell.

Not this. This made her feel sad.

"Try another one," suggested the fairy.
The next card Mya pulled out said:
FEELING SAD? WHY NOT TALK ABOUT IT?
"Okay," said Mya to the fairy, "I was hoping for a magic spell, but you gave me something that just feels really hard."

"It gets easier," said the fairy, kindly. "Go back to how you were feeling today at school."

Mya thought about how worried she felt when she didn't understand the math problem.
She pulled out another card.

FEELING WORRIED? TAKE FIVE DEEP BREATHS.

"Hey, that sounds easy!" said Mya.

"And it works!" replied the fairy.

Mya thought about how mad she felt when Isabella laughed at her. She pulled out a card.

FEELING MAD? COUNT TO TEN IN YOUR HEAD.

"Okay, I can do that!" said Mya, starting to smile.

"Remember," the fairy said, "no one else can see your backpack, or your Magic Methods. Only you. But if you use the Methods, they will help you. Be happy!" And she disappeared in a mini puff of glitter.

Mya thought about how she had hurt her mom's feelings. It had made her feel very sad.
She pulled out a card.

SAYING SORRY MAKES YOU FEEL BETTER, TOO!
the card told her.

She went downstairs to find her mom.

The next day, Mya felt tired again.
But instead of being mad at her mom, she
remembered the Method:

WHY NOT TALK ABOUT IT?
So she told her mom how she felt.

"Oh, honey!" said her mom, "We'll have to find
a way to help you sleep better. Maybe a bath before
bed would help. We can try different ways until we
find one that works for you."

At school, Mya couldn't understand her history lesson.

She started to feel worried.

The feeling grew **bigger** and **bigger**.

She took five deep breaths.

The feeling got smaller, and then it went away.

Isabella wasn't talking to her.

Mya remembered how she had made things better with her mom.

"Isabella," she whispered, "I'm sorry I broke your pencil.

I was feeling tired and worried."

Isabella beamed at her. "That's okay, Mya.

I know you were feeling down. I'm sorry I laughed at you."

"So, do you understand what's going on in this lesson?" whispered Mya.

"Not even a little bit," smiled Isabella.

They both laughed.

And that's how Mya got her Magic Methods for dealing with feelings that are too strong.

Lightning Source UK Ltd.
Milton Keynes UK
UKHW050727181222
414072UK00003B/37